# THE REVENGE OF ISHTAR

RETOLD AND ILLUSTRATED BY LUDMILA ZEMAN

TUNDRA BOOKS

THE CITY OF URUK had become the happiest place in the ancient world.

Gilgamesh, once the cruelest and loneliest of kings, had changed.
He had learned through friendship with Enkidu, the wild man from the forest,
how to be human and care for others.

With Enkidu to help him, Gilgamesh worked to make Uruk
a good city for all who lived there.
By day they sailed on the Euphrates River and made plans.
They directed the building of fine houses and magnificent temples.

On quiet evenings, they played the game of twenty squares
while the beautiful Shamhat sang and watched.
Everyone loved Shamhat. She had brought Enkidu to Uruk
and peace to the city. People passing outside the palace
stopped to listen to her voice and were grateful.

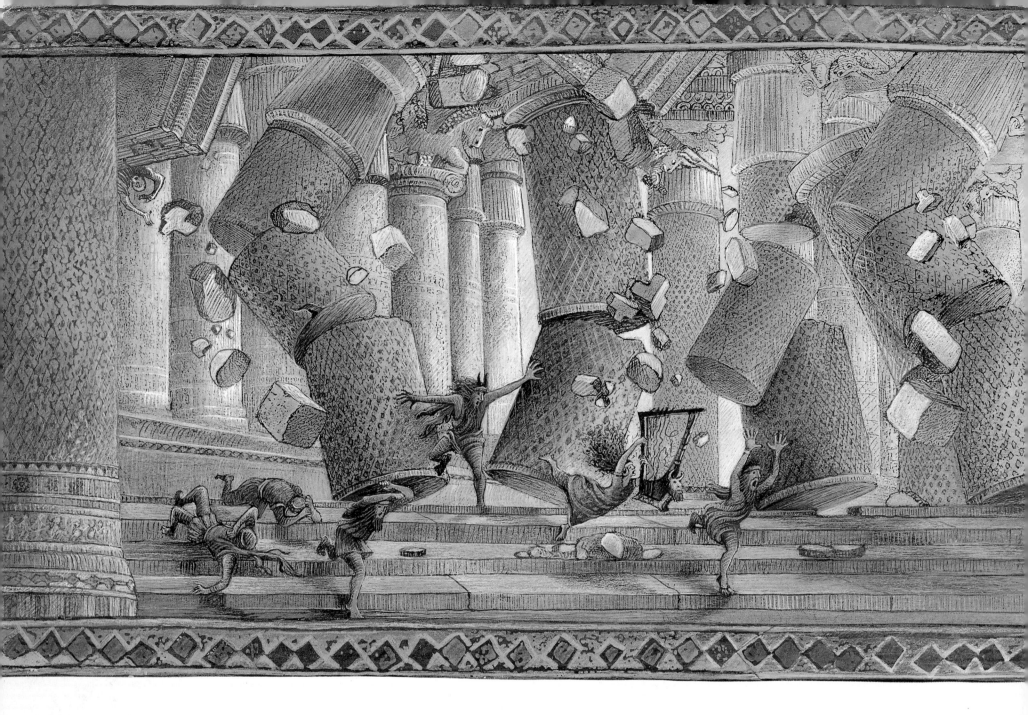

B UT THE PEACE and joy did not last.
One evening without warning, terror struck. Pillars crashed down. Roofs fell in.
People ran in panic. Enkidu saw Shamhat cry for help. He rushed to save her. But he was too late.
He lifted her lifeless body, carried her to Gilgamesh and cried in despair: "Why?"

"IT IS THE MONSTER Humbaba," Gilgamesh raged. "He hides in the mountains. We must destroy him before he comes again. If you will not come with me, I will go alone. I am not afraid of death."

"I am afraid," Enkidu answered. "We will face dangers from which we may never return."

Then he looked at the beautiful Shamhat and overcame his fear. "I will go with you," he said.

GILGAMESH ordered the finest armor, swords, spears and axes to be made.
The people of Uruk knew the dangerous mission their king and Enkidu were undertaking.
They came to the gates to watch them leave and wish them victory and a safe return.
The two set out for the distant mountains in a royal chariot led by wild asses.

THE VAST LONELY desert lay ahead. For a long week they traveled.
The sun burned by day. Violent winds chilled by night. Bad dreams came to trouble Gilgamesh.
He dreamed a mountain fell on them, that the earth split open and swallowed them,
that fire rained from the sky. Each night Enkidu comforted him until they reached the mountains.

A THICK FOREST of cedars blocked their way. They left their chariot and continued on foot.
They cut trees to clear a path. As they reached the foot of the mountain they heard Humbaba roar:
"Why have you come here, Gilgamesh? I will tear you apart and feed your flesh to the vultures."
Out of a crater on the mountaintop Humbaba the monster rose, breathing fire and smoke.

LIGHTNING FLASHED and thunder roared. Stones and ashes descended, blinding them. Gilgamesh felt giant claws around his waist and the monster Humbaba lifted him to the sky. Then, suddenly, as if the gods came to help, winds blew away the smoke and Humbaba's face appeared. With all his strength, Gilgamesh thrust his spear between the monster's open jaws.

THE EARTH SHOOK as Humbaba fell, snarling. Gilgamesh and Enkidu swung their axes.
As they stood beside the dead monster, the goddess Ishtar arrived in a chariot with winged horses.
"Gilgamesh," she said. "It was I who sent the winds to help you. Come with me and be my husband.
You shall have a chariot of gold. The kings of the earth will bow down and kiss your feet."

"Go away, Ishtar," Gilgamesh answered. "You do not tempt me with your riches or power. I have built a great city and I will not leave it. My people love me and I honor them. I have a friend who is ready to give his life for me. I need nothing more."

Ishtar's eyes blazed. "You dare reject me?" She rode off in a fury of hate.

GILGAMESH and Enkidu returned to Uruk as heroes. All the city turned out to welcome them. But they had no time to enjoy their victory. The sky opened and Ishtar came back in revenge.

S HE HAD HARNESSED the Bull of Heaven, the monstrous beast of the skies, and she rode it to Uruk.
Its shadow fell upon the city, spreading fear and panic.

ISHTAR WATCHED from the wall as the bull crashed through Uruk.
Its hoofs smashed buildings. Its tail swept stones and bricks away like dust. Its snort opened pits
as if an earthquake had struck. Men tried to stop it and were crushed under falling rock.
Only Enkidu, remembering what he knew of animals, managed to get close.

HE APPROACHED the bull from its side so he would not be seen. As the giant tail swung toward him he caught it, pulled himself onto the beast's back and grabbed the horns.
Ishtar screamed from the wall as the bull thrashed about wildly, trying to throw Enkidu off.
Enkidu hung on with all his strength. The bull snorted and leaped over the city wall.

ISHTAR could not believe what she was seeing. She ran along the wall, shouting.
As the bull landed, Gilgamesh jumped directly in front and stood facing it.
The bull stopped in surprise, just long enough for Enkidu to jump off and grab its tail.
With all his might Enkidu pulled the bull back and Gilgamesh swung his sword.

ISHTAR'S SCREAM cut the skies as she saw Gilgamesh kill the bull.
For a second time, Gilgamesh had gone against her. Now he would be a greater hero than ever.
"I will find a way to hurt you!" she yelled. "I will not rest until you are punished."
"Do not threaten my friend!" Enkidu shouted back. He cut off the bull's tail and threw it at her.

GILGAMESH and Enkidu celebrated, proud and pleased at what they had achieved. Ishtar felt the bull's tail weighing on her neck like a disgrace. She began to plot her final revenge.

THE PEOPLE OF URUK gathered outside the wall to see the beast that had spread so much terror.
They sang the praises of their king and his friend for again saving them from monsters.

S INCE MONSTER beasts of earth or heaven could not hurt Gilgamesh, Ishtar found another way.
She sent a terrible illness upon Enkidu. Day by day, he seemed to waste away into sleep.
Gilgamesh tried desperately to wake him. "Do not leave me now, dear friend," he begged, weeping.
"Together we fought monsters and won. There is more for us to do." But Enkidu did not wake.

ALL URUK MOURNED. Gilgamesh built a tomb to his friend. One evening as he knelt there, Shamhat came back as a bird to take Enkidu's spirit to the Underworld, but Enkidu protested: "Why did you bring me to this city to die? I was happy in the forest before I met you." Shamhat replied: "Here you found friendship few ever know. And the lasting love of a people."

As ENKIDU and Shamhat flew into the night,
King Gilgamesh went out alone onto the river.

"Death is the worst monster in the world,"
he thought. "It has taken Enkidu from me.
Someday it will take me from my people.
I must find a way to destroy it.
I must seek out the secret of immortality."

"That will be my last quest."

The story of Gilgamesh is one of the oldest stories in the world; it was inscribed onto clay tablets over 5000 years ago in Mesopotamia (where Iraq and Syria are today). The epic tells us much about the life of the people in that ancient land, their beliefs and the world around them. The forest that Gilgamesh and Enkidu must travel through on their way to meet the monster Humbaba has been identified as one in northern Syria. The monster might have been a volcano in the mountains that run from Anatolia to Armenia, and the Bull of Heaven is thought to personify a drought of seven years, supposedly sent by Ishtar when Gilgamesh rejected her. Later, scribes in other parts of Mesopotamia changed the drought into a bull.

The board game played by Gilgamesh and Enkidu at the opening of the book (and that decorates the endleaves) was excavated by British archaeologists and is now in the British Museum in London. It has several names, including the Royal Game of Ur, the Game of Twenty Squares and Pack of Dogs. Even though all the parts to the game were found no one is quite sure of the exact rules.

Mesopotamia was one of the world's first civilizations. The land between the Tigris and Euphrates rivers is now mostly desert, but in ancient times it was very fertile. When the ancient peoples started farming these lands over 8000 years ago, the extra food they produced eventually allowed the building of towns and then cities with names like Nippur, Ur, Lagash and Uruk — where a king by the name of Gilgamesh once reigned, and the ruins of the famous wall can still be seen.

Clay tablets were first found in the earth of Iraq and Syria by French and British archaeologists in the 19th century. They brought the tablets home with them, and others deciphered the cuneiform writing later in the century. Today similar tablets continue to be found and can be seen in many museums but those containing the Gilgamesh story are rare. The collections in London, Paris, Philadelphia and Berlin (where the Ishtar Gate has been reconstructed) are especially famous.

I would like to thank my children Linda and Malvina for their help and support.

— *Ludmila Zeman*

©1993 Ludmila Zeman

Published in Canada by Tundra Books, Montreal, Quebec H3Z 2N2

Published in the United States by Tundra Books of Northern New York, Plattsburgh, N.Y. 12901

Library of Congress Catalog Number: 93-60332

The publisher has applied funds from its Canada Council block grant for 1993 toward the editing and production of this book.

**Canadian Cataloging in Publication Data:**

Zeman, Ludmila
    The Revenge of Ishtar
For children.
ISBN 0-88776-315-4
    I. Title.
PS8599.E492R49 1993      jC813'54      C93-090203-3
PZ7.Z45Re 1993

The artist wishes to thank Dr. Irving Finkel, Assistant Keeper, Department of Western Asiatic Antiquities, The British Museum, London, for his kind assistance.

Design by Dan O'Leary.

Printed in Hong Kong by South China Printing Co. Ltd.